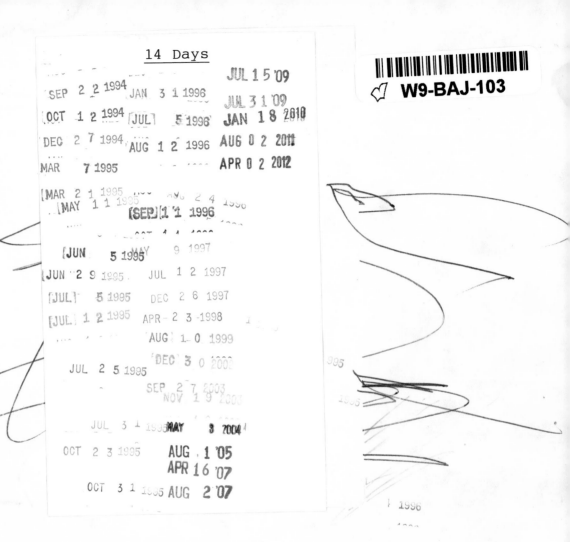

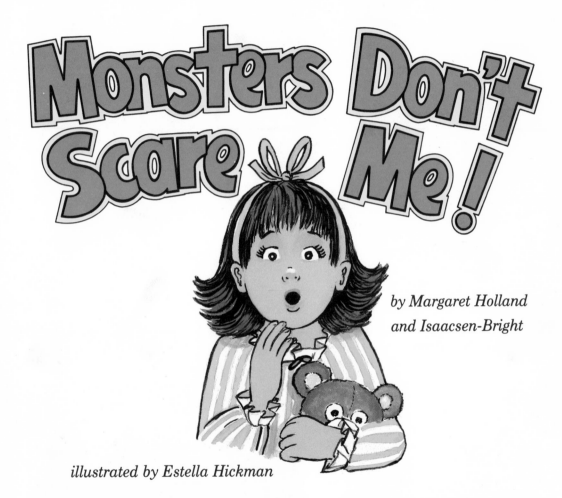

Monsters Don't Scare Me!

*by Margaret Holland
and Isaacsen-Bright*

illustrated by Estella Hickman

MONSTERS DON'T SCARE ME is one of a series of Predictable Read Together Books edited by Dr. Margaret Holland. Books in this series are designed to help young children begin to read naturally and easily. See back cover for additional information.

To Jimmy Fiala, who can.

Published by Willowisp Press, Inc.
401 E. Wilson Bridge Road, Worthington, Ohio 43085

Copyright ©1988 by Willowisp Press, Inc.

Printed in the United States of America

10 9 8 7 6 5 4 3

ISBN 0-87406-256-X

"You're ready to walk to school by yourself," my dad said.
"Do you think you can do it?"
I'm afraid I can't do it. What if I get lost?
What if the light never changes, and I can't cross the street?

40802

What if a big hairy monster grabs me?

I hope I can do it!
I think I can do it!
I know I can do it!

I DID IT! I DID!

"It's time to dive off the diving board," my swim teacher said.
"Do you think you can do it?"
I'm afraid I can't do it. What if I do a belly flop?
What if I have to crawl back off of the board?

What if a slimy sea monster grabs me?

I hope I can do it!
I think I can do it!
I know I can do it!

I DID IT! I DID!

"It's time for your dance recital," my dance teacher said.
"Do you think you can do it?"
I'm afraid I can't do it. What if everyone laughs at me?
What if my costume falls off?

What if a scary monster trips me?

I hope I can do it!
I think I can do it!
I know I can do it!

I DID IT! I DID!

"Let's go sledding!" my brother said.
"Can you go to the basement and bring up the sled?"
I'm afraid I can't do it. What if the lights go out?
What if the door closes, and I can't get out?

What if the basement monster gets me?

I hope I can do it! I think I can do it!
I know I can do it!

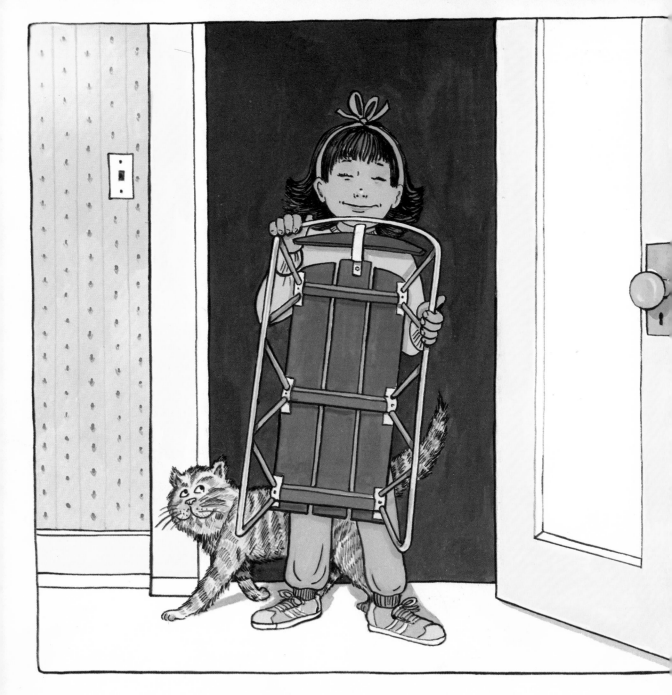

I DID IT! I DID!

"I'd like you to take this note to the principal," my teacher said.
"Do you think you can find your way there and back?"
I'm afraid I can't do it. What if I lose the note?
What if I can't find my way there?

What if there's a monster in the principal's office?

I hope I can do it!
I think I can do it!
I know I can do it!

I DID IT! I DID!

"Let's read this book again," my mother said.
"Do you think you can do it?"
What if there's a monster at the end of this book?

j 40802

I hope I can do it!
I think I can do it! I know I can do it!
I DID IT! I DID!
Monsters don't scare me.